The ALABAMA Night Before Christmas

E.J. Sullivan

Illustrated by
Ernie Eldredge

SWEET WATER PRESS

The Alabama Night Before Christmas
© 2005 by Sweetwater Press
Produced by Cliff Road Books

ISBN 1-58173-341-0

Printed in China

The ALABAMA
Night Before
Christmas

'Twas an Alabama night before Christmas,
　and from Mentone to Dothan
Not a creature was stirring —
　even Vulcan was snorin'.

Our stockings were hung
    on the glass sliding doors,
Near the sand-dollar wind chimes
    Mom got in Gulf Shores.

Baby Sister was snuggled all safe in her bed
With visions of cheerleader stuff in her head.
And me in my Bama jammies, and Luke in his War Eagles,
Were just settling in with Buck and Buster, our beagles.

When out by the gas grill I heard a noise
   you wouldn't believe –
It was louder than our tailgate party
   on Iron Bowl Eve!

I sprang to the window
and threw open the shutter
Armed with Dad's new autographed
Hubert Green putter!

The moon was as bright as the new Dollar Store
They put in down the road – it's open all hours!
And then what to my wondering eyes should I spy
But a Marshall Space rocket blazing on by!

With a little old driver
so lively 'n' quick,
He coulda won Talladega
ten times in a lick!

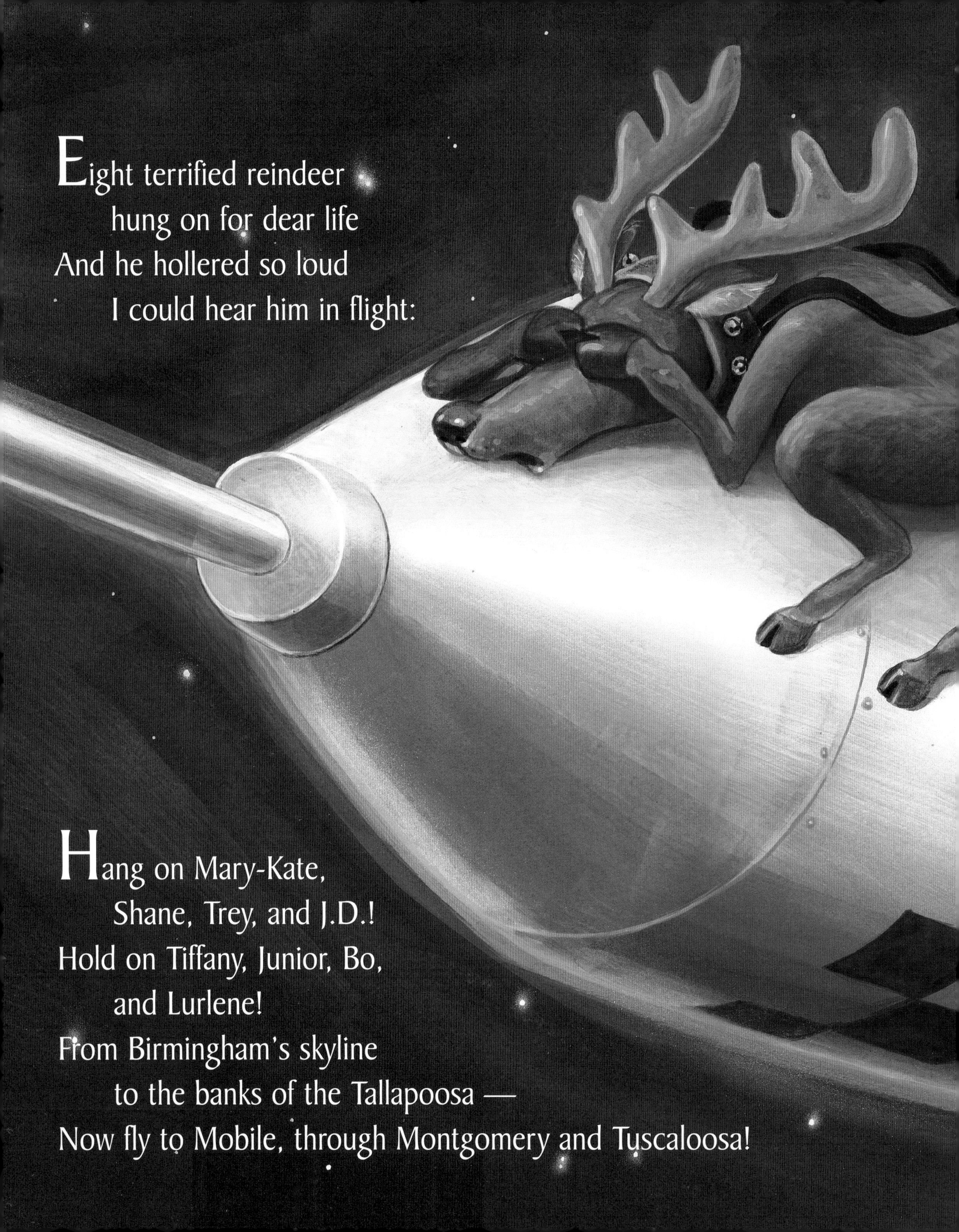

Eight terrified reindeer
    hung on for dear life
And he hollered so loud
    I could hear him in flight:

Hang on Mary-Kate,
    Shane, Trey, and J.D.!
Hold on Tiffany, Junior, Bo,
    and Lurlene!
From Birmingham's skyline
    to the banks of the Tallapoosa —
Now fly to Mobile, through Montgomery and Tuscaloosa!

Yⁿou know when the Doppler Radar comes on TV
Showing how tornadoes are gonna blow us all away?
Well that's how this rocketship made the sky look —
Got me so worked up I needed a Buffalo Rock!

As I finished my drink I saw our magnolia tree shake
When the bottom of that rocketship started to scrape.
I looked up through the limbs and caught him red-handed —
On our DeSoto Caverns birdhouse Santa'd crash landed!

Bless his heart. He looked bigger than Ruben to me,
With hair white as Stabler's, tangled up in that tree.
Mom's always saying I should help folks who are older
So I helped him get down onto our John Deere mower.

Santa headed inside
in two licks and a shake
And filled all our stockings
with Little Debbie cakes.

Then he looked right at me,
    and before goin' out the door
Slapped on top of the TV
    some new bass fishing lures.

He fired up his rocket and soon they were gone,
All the while telling those deer to hang on.
But I heard him holler out as his rig sped away,
"Merry Christmas, Alabama!
        I wish I could stay!"